Dedicated to my brave little Dutch nephews,
Liam and Rohan – A.A.

To Harvey and Megan
and their great imaginations – P.K.

Chapter 1:
George the Soldier

George was a soldier, strong and brave.
He rode a huge white horse called Bayard.
Together they rode through the land, helping
people wherever they could. His servant,
Burak, followed behind, driving the cart
that carried George's armour and all
their supplies.

One day they rode into the countryside,
Bayard swishing his fine, thick tail.
Suddenly George saw the king and all
his people out on the hillside.
Everyone was weeping and wailing.
"What's wrong?" he asked.

"My daughter is in great danger," the king cried. "The dragon is going to eat her!" George saw bones all over the hillside.

"What's been happening here?" asked George.

Chapter 2:
The Dragon's Demands

"The only water for our town comes from a fresh spring. There is enough cool, clear water there for all of us," said the king.

"But one day a huge dragon arrived. He's stayed here ever since and guards the spring fiercely. He won't let us have any water unless we feed him every day. He's already gobbled up all our sheep and goats."

7

"Now the dragon demands a young girl to eat every day, before he lets us take water from the spring," the king explained.
"When he's eaten all the juicy young girls he'll start on the boys," screeched a woman.
"Then, when they are all gone, he'll start on tough old people like us."
"Please help us, Sir George!" begged the townspeople.

"There was nothing else we could do! To be fair, we had a lottery to see who would be eaten first. The name of the princess came out first!"

"Please fight that wicked dragon,"
begged the king. "Otherwise the
princess and all of us will die!"

"I will help you and fight this greedy
monster," said brave George.
Burak helped him put on his sturdy armour.
Then George picked up his weapons, his
long lance and his sharp sword.

11

Chapter 3:
Fighting the Dragon

George rode Bayard to the spring just below the town. The princess was amazed to see a knight in shining armour ride past her on a huge white horse.

The townspeople watched from a safe distance. They didn't want to be eaten before their time. They didn't want to be eaten at all! If the dragon got Sir George they had to be ready to run.

The foulest odour that George had ever smelt filled the air. But the dragon was nowhere to be seen.

Suddenly there was a boom like angry thunder. The gigantic dragon soared down upon him from the sky. Its vast green wings blocked out the sun but George could still see the many rows of sharp teeth that glistened in the creature's open mouth.

George's horse rose up on his hind legs as the dragon swooped down. A great burst of flame shot from the dragon's mouth, just missing George's head.

Bayard's fine white tail was sizzled like a burnt sausage.

George swiftly aimed his lance at the dragon's body and charged towards the smoking, raging beast. He wanted to send the weapon straight through the evil monster's heart.

The dragon's shimmering scales were as hard as steel plates. George's lance crumbled into a thousand pieces. He was thrown to the ground and immediately Bayard raced for the safety of the town.

George rolled under a tree and drew his
sword, thinking of the poor princess.
He must find a way to defeat this mighty
dragon once and for all.

Chapter 4:
The Dragon's Weakness

Another burst of flames set the tree ablaze and the heat cracked the soldier's armour wide open.

Now George had nothing to protect him from the heat and flames ...

nor from the dragon's terrible teeth, which looked as if they could bite through steel.

George curled himself into a small ball and rolled into a rocky area on the hillside. Without any armour, what could he do? George hid amongst the rocks.
Did the dragon have a weak spot?
Or would George be eaten as well as the princess and the rest of the townspeople?

The dragon bellowed as it lost sight of its prey. It prowled around the rocks, but George was well hidden. The dragon was so close that a single fiery breath could have made him look like a piece of burnt toast.

Standing just above him, the dragon lifted its mighty wings to soar into the sky and search for George.

The soldier saw just what he was looking for. Brave George climbed out and crept across the rocks. He was hidden from the dragon's eyes beneath its own huge wing.

He leapt out and thrust his sword right under the dragon's wing. This is a dragon's only weak spot. There are no scales to protect the dragon there and the blade went straight into its heart.

George leapt back, away from the dragon's putrid breath and heaving wings.

Dark blood burst forth and stained the ground as the dragon's roar changed to a choking cry. Then the creature's body thudded to the ground.

The dragon was dead and the princess and all the townspeople were saved.

Immediately George ran down the hill and untied the princess. Another roar was heard in the land. But this time it was the joyful sound of everyone cheering as George brought the princess back to her father.

Chapter 5:
A New Beginning

The people of the town rejoiced for days.
The king told the blacksmith to make
George a new set of armour and weapons.
They were even better than the ones the
dragon had destroyed, silver and shining.
He also gave George a huge bag of
gold as a reward.

The princess bathed the sizzled stump of Bayard's tail and even offered her own hair to replace it.

"Thank you, but it will soon grow back!" laughed George.

George used the bag of gold to buy more sheep and goats for the people of the town. Now, who else needed his help? He and Burak loaded the shiny new armour into the cart and saddled up Bayard. Then the brave soldier went quietly on his way.

29

About the story

George and the Dragon is a legend which is part of Christian tradition – St George is the patron saint of England, as well as of Georgia and of Moscow, Russia. The story is Eastern in origin and the setting is thought to be Libya. It was brought to England by the Crusaders – knights who fought to spread the Christian religion throughout the world. We don't know very much about the real St George, but it is thought that he was killed because he refused to persecute the Christians in 303 CE on 23 April. St George's Day is celebrated on this date every year. The legend about the dragon killing comes from much later in the Middle Ages around the 12th century CE.

Be in the story!

Imagine you are
the princess and your name
has just been chosen
to be fed to the dragon.
What will you say to
your father?

Now imagine that you
are a reporter. You must
write the story of the
princess's rescue for
the local newspaper.
Include some quotes
from the princess, the
king and George!

First published in 2014 by
Franklin Watts
338 Euston Road
London
NW1 3BH

Franklin Watts Australia
Level 17/207 Kent Street
Sydney
NSW 2000

A CIP catalogue record for this book is available
from the British Library.

The artwork for this story first appeared in
Hopscotch Adventures: George and the Dragon

ISBN 978 1 4451 3001 9 (hbk)
ISBN 978 1 4451 3004 0 (pbk)
ISBN 978 1 4451 3003 3 (library ebook)
ISBN 978 1 4451 3002 6 (ebook)

Series Editor: Jackie Hamley
Series Advisor: Catherine Glavina
Series Designer: Cathryn Gilbert

Printed in China

Franklin Watts is a divison of
Hachette Children's Books,
an Hachette UK company.
www.hachette.co.uk